Disney PRINCESS

Magical Worlds

Disney PRESS

Los Angeles • New York

dressing screen

vanity

Happy birthday!

Jaq

Gus

bluebirds

washbowl

trunk

Surprise!

Bruno

ribbon

sewing basket

book

Once upon a time, Cinderella lived with her wicked stepfamily in a château, and did chores all day long. Fortunately, her attic bedroom provided the perfect escape for her and her animal friends.

Cinderella never gave up on her dreams, and now she lives in the kingdom's beautiful castle with her true love! They're not the only ones celebrating—the King and Cinderella's mouse friends are happy, too.

the King

the Grand Duke

Goodbye, Cinderelly!

mice

the Fairy Godmother

wedding slipper

staircase

When Snow White needed a place to go, she found a home—and friendship—with the Seven Dwarfs. All the activities they enjoyed together made their cottage a very special place.

After Tiana turned into a frog, she traveled through the enchanting Louisiana bayou to break the spell. Her journey with Prince Naveen led them to some beautiful spots—and to becoming human again!

fireflies

You just kissed yourself a princess!

Prince Naveen

birds

Tiana

flowers

water lilies

swamp

trees

Juju   Mama Odie

deer

Louis

beaver

turtles

raccoon

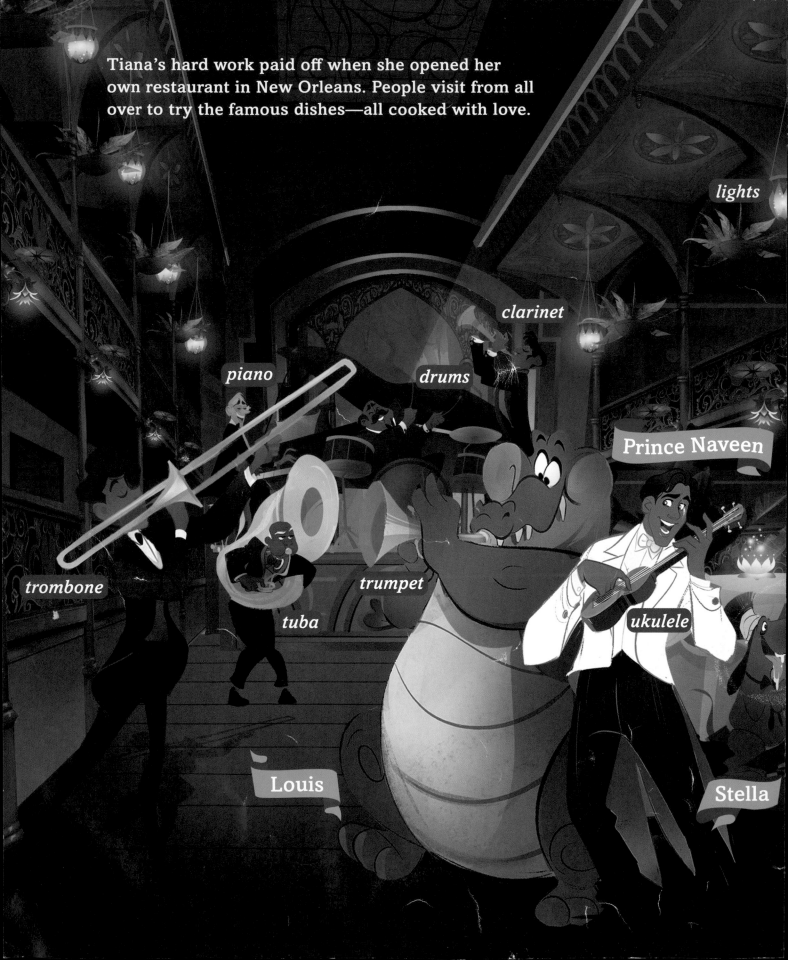

Tiana's hard work paid off when she opened her own restaurant in New Orleans. People visit from all over to try the famous dishes—all cooked with love.

lights

clarinet

piano

drums

Prince Naveen

trombone

tuba

trumpet

ukulele

Louis

Stella

Don't you loose another arrow!

King Fergus

Queen Elinor

dancers

Young MacGuffin

dog

target

Lord MacGuffin

Lord Macintosh

Wee and Lord
Dingwall

Young Macintosh

Merida didn't miss a chance to show off her archery skills at Castle DunBroch's Highland Games. All the clans of the kingdom gathered for the event—and so did Merida's parents and three little brothers.

Pascal

painting

curtain

Rapunzel

Almost finished!

paints and brushes

guitar

Rapunzel's hair

Rapunzel used to spend her days in a tall tower, watching the floating lanterns from her window and wondering when her life would begin. But she and her friend, Pascal, still found ways to pass the time.

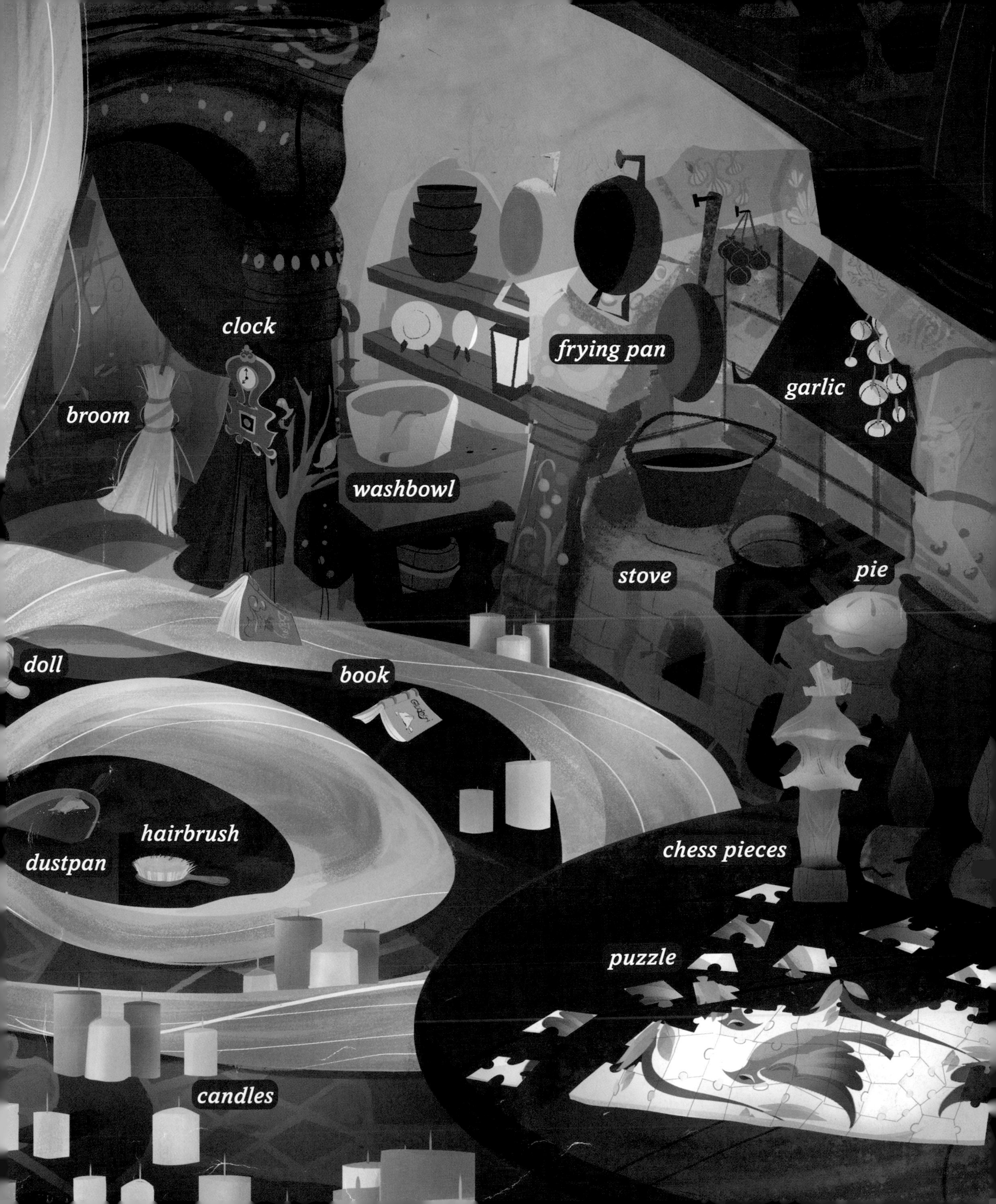

clock

broom

frying pan

garlic

washbowl

stove

pie

doll

book

dustpan

hairbrush

chess pieces

puzzle

candles

Rapunzel finally discovered her true home in the kingdom! As the princess, she enjoys the many festivities, and best of all, she finally sees the lanterns in person with the one she loves.

Are you ready to see the lights?

Flynn Rider

Rapunzel

musicians

violin

andolin

sun

hair braiders

chimney

woodcutter's cottage

cupcake

Fauna

window

dress

wand

Don't go too far!

Flora

Merryweather

Before she pricked her finger on the spindle, Aurora lived in a cottage with her three guardians. In this forest haven, hidden magic surrounded her—even when she didn't know it.

For a long time, Princess Jasmine could only dream of what Agrabah's bustling marketplace looked like. Then she snuck out from behind the palace walls to get a closer look.

bananas

pears

dates

pistachios   oranges

jewelry

pottery

When Jasmine was caught taking an apple to give to a boy, Aladdin helped her escape. He took her up to his hideout and showed off his view of the palace. As they talked, they both admitted they felt . . . trapped.

the Sultan's palace

Agrabah

mountains

Oh, it's wonderful.

buildings

Jasmine

pillows

rug

In the underwater kingdom of Atlantica, Ariel would daydream while her six older sisters performed in concert.

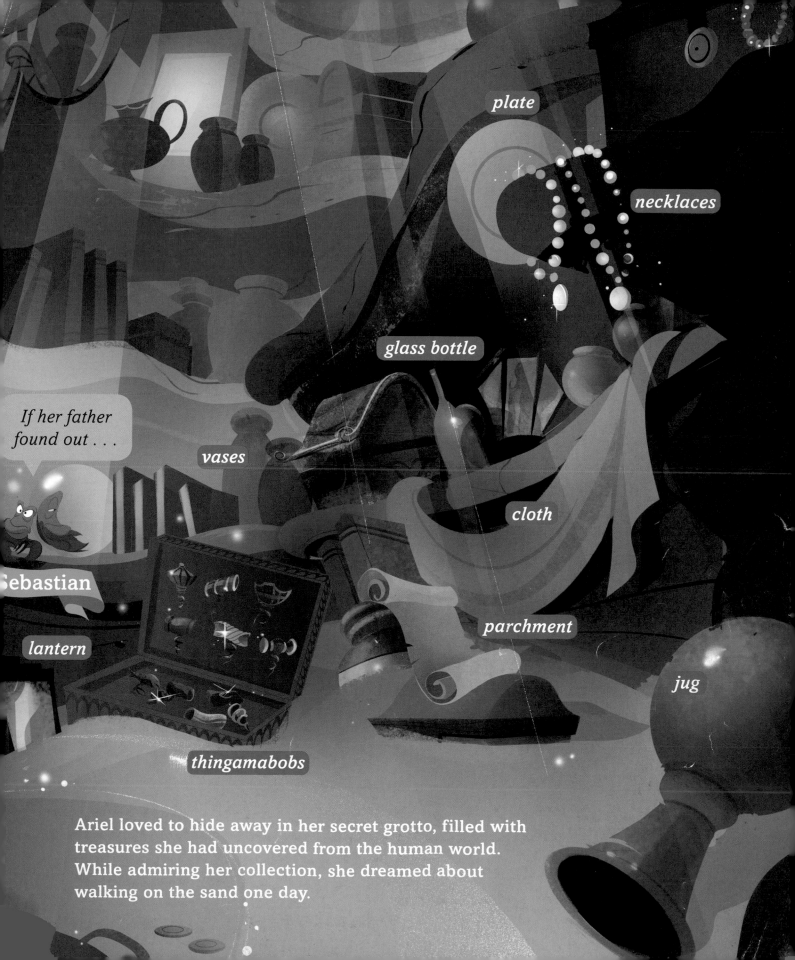

plate

necklaces

glass bottle

If her father found out . . .

vases

cloth

Sebastian

parchment

lantern

jug

thingamabobs

Ariel loved to hide away in her secret grotto, filled with treasures she had uncovered from the human world. While admiring her collection, she dreamed about walking on the sand one day.

ocahontas loved spending time in the forest outside her village, listening to the wind. She hoped it would one day lead her to answers about her future.

waterfall

turtles

rainbow

Flit

Let's explore a
new path today.

Meeko

mother's necklace

Pocahontas

canoe

oar

river

Chip
This all looks delicious!
Belle
cheese soufflé
blueberry pie
Mrs. Potts
sugar bowls
Lumiere

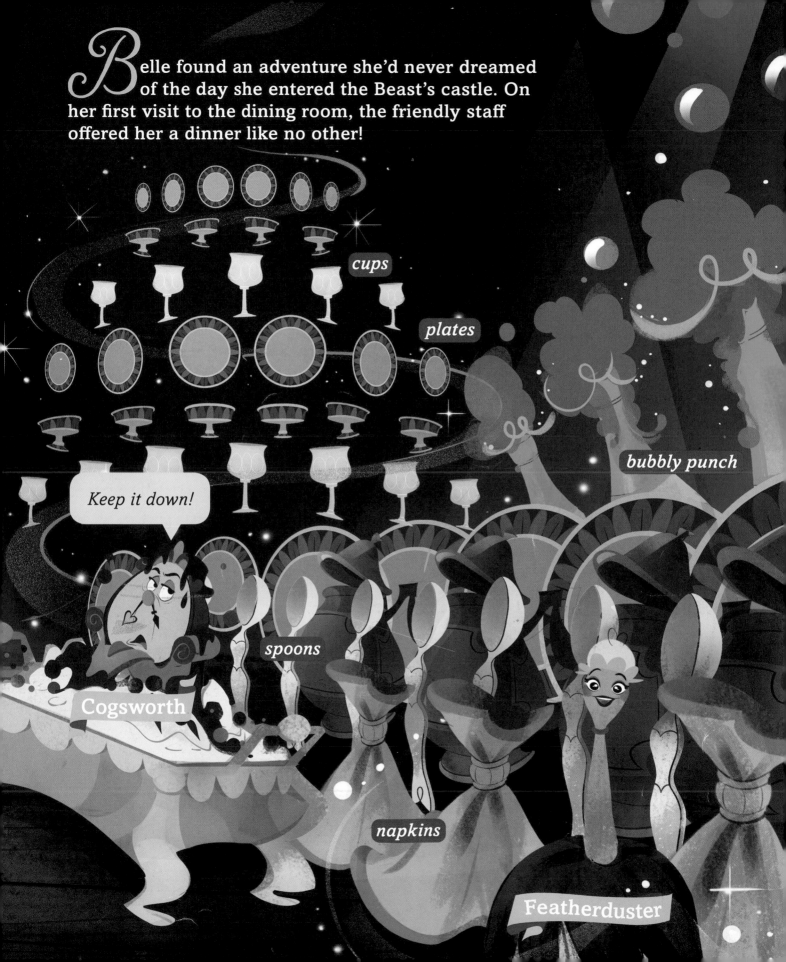

Belle found an adventure she'd never dreamed of the day she entered the Beast's castle. On her first visit to the dining room, the friendly staff offered her a dinner like no other!

cups

plates

bubbly punch

Keep it down!

spoons

Cogsworth

napkins

Featherduster

Belle came to see the caring heart beneath the Beast's gruffness—especially after they shared an unforgettable dance in the castle ballroom.

chandelier

windows

the Beast

Belle

ball gown

After courageous Mulan saved China, her heart led her back to the Fa family home. Her family welcomed her and her new friends with love and laughter.

magnolia tree

moon gate

Li Shang

Khan

Mushu

Cri-Kee

Grandmother Fa

water lilies

pond

oana grew up on the island of Motunui, and while she often dreamed of exploring beyond its shores, she also trained to succeed her father as the village chief.

The water kept calling to Moana, and she
answered it by going on an adventure. Now, as
a master wayfinder, she leads her people across
the sea, searching for new islands to explore!

Maui
as a hawk

sails

canoes

ocean

manta ray

With magic, friendship, and adventure around every corner, it's no wonder the princesses' worlds are worth visiting over and over again!

Designed by Catalina Castro and Margaret Peng

Illustrated by Nicoletta Baldari

Special thanks to Jean-Paul Orpinas, Hali Baumstein, and Samantha McFerrin

Copyright © 2021 Disney Enterprises, Inc.

The movie *The Princess and the Frog* Copyright © 2009 Disney, story inspired in part by the book *The Frog Princess* by E. D. Baker Copyright © 2002, published by Bloomsbury Publishing, Inc.

Printed in the United States of America

First Hardcover Edition, August 2021

1 3 5 7 9 10 8 6 4 2

ISBN 978-1-368-04522-3

FAC-034274-21169

Library of Congress Control Number: 2020937025